Habitat and habits

Common hideouts
- Under sinks and desks
- In metal cans and dumpsters
- Along streets
- In public places

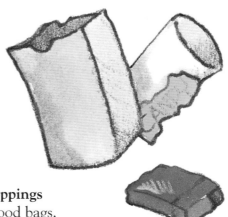

Tracks and droppings
Scattered fast-food bags, candy wrappers, foam cups, cigarette packs, broken toys, and household objects

Hibernation
Sleeps underground for years in landfills, but may wake at any time and escape into water or air

Favorite foods
- Bottles and cans
- Paper and plastics
- Junk mail
- Food scraps
(but will eat anything humans waste)

Migration routes
Travels with flies or litterbugs and always follows people

Special powers
- Stinking
- Looking ugly
- Spreading disease

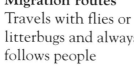

Dangers
- Sharp claws
- Broken, pointy teeth
- Germs

Weakness
Shrinks when it sees this symbol

Behavior
Attacks are rare. When a human comes near, a garbage monster usually lies still and smells bad. As soon as the human goes away, the monster continues to rot and spread.

the GARBAGE monster

Words by Joni Sensel
Pictures by Christopher L. Bivins

First Edition

dream factory

Dream Factory Books
Enumclaw, Washington
www.DreamFactoryBooks.com

The Garbage Monster

Written by Joni Sensel
Illustrated by Christopher L. Bivins

Dream Factory Books
P.O. Box 874
Enumclaw, Washington, 98022, USA
www.DreamFactoryBooks.com
877-377-7030

Printed in Hong Kong
5 4 3 2 1

Publisher's Cataloguing-in-Publication Data
Sensel, Joni, 1962-
    The garbage monster / words by Joni Sensel, pictures
by Christopher L. Bivins. -- 1st ed.
      p. cm.
    SUMMARY: Jo didn't like to take out the family garbage, and it piled up until the garbage came to life and took Jo out! The monster was ugly, smelly, and buzzing with litterbugs, but Jo successfully disposed of him, bit by bit--and now she takes the garbage out promptly!
    Audience: Ages 4-8.
    Audience: Pre-K--3rd grade.
    LCCN: 00-110316
    ISBN: 0-9701195-2-6

    1. Refuse and refuse disposal--Juvenile fiction. 2. Monsters--Juvenile fiction. 3. Recycling (Waste, etc.) --Juvenile fiction. 4. Stories in rhyme.   I. Bivins, Christopher, 1961- ill. II. Title.

    PZ8.3.S468Gar 2001   [E]
            QBI00-901835

Artful Dragon Press
Seattle, Washington / Hong Kong

For my brother Tom and sister Sherry,
who always encouraged me in my
endeavors, artistic and otherwise
— *C.L.B.*

For my mom and dad
and for the Handful of Writers
— *J.J.S.*

"Jo, take out the garbage!"

…my mom would often shout.

Pretending not to hear, I'd mutter,
"It can take itself out."

ur house had tons of garbage:
cans and bottles, plastic bags,
bones and boxes, broken toys,
and loads of dirty rags.

I never gave the trash a thought,
but made more than I should:
I threw away all kinds of things
that really were still good.

But one night I was startled
by a messy mystery —
when I was slow to take the trash,

the *garbage*
took out *me!*

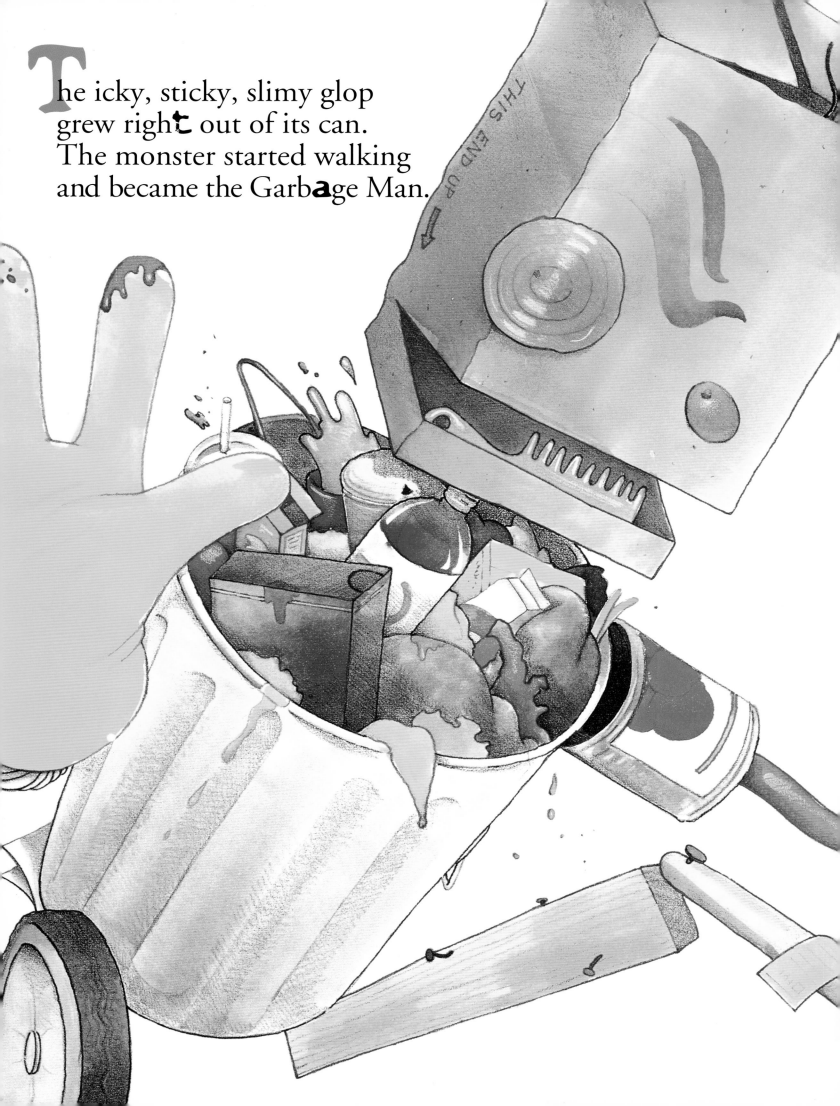

The icky, sticky, slimy glop
grew right out of its can.
The monster started walking
and became the Garbage Man.

He didn't look too pleasant
and P.U., did he stink!
He faintly buzzed with litterbugs.
His growling made me blink.

He dropped me flat in my front yard
and got down on one knee
and grumbled with his smelly breath,
"You fed me, now I'm free!

"I'll scatter rubbish near and far —
I'll start here on your street!
I'll fill the yards and foul the parks!
Ha! Nothing will stay neat!"

'll tell you, I was kinda scared.
You would've been scared too.
This slob was talking trash at me —
But what could one kid do?

And then I took a closer look
and jumped up, proud and tall,
and shouted, "Oh, you silly junk!
You aren't *garbage* at all!"

With that I pulled the cardboard box
right off his swollen head.
"I'll use this to pack up some things
and put them in the shed."

Next I pulled the paper
from the monster's big backside.
"And this I still can write on,
so I'll take it back inside.

"These leaves and grass and bits of food
can make the garden grow,
and I'll give these useful gadgets
to a charity I know."

he bottles, jars, and cans he wore
all fit the recycling bin,
and so the monster dwindled.
I flashed a gleeful grin.

I stuffed him in a trash bag,
twisted it up tight,
and slammed the lid on what was left.
He went without a fight.

Since then our trash goes hungry
and gets smaller every day,
and when it's time to take it out,
I do it right away!

Garbage Monster
Trashicus Stinkimus

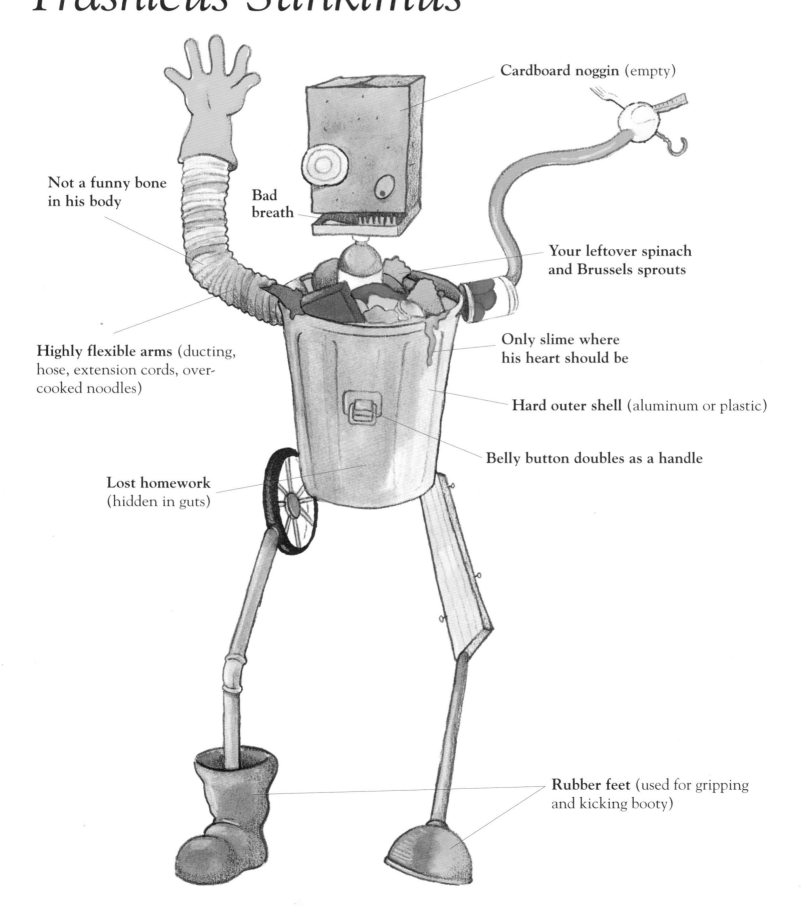

Cardboard noggin (empty)

Not a funny bone in his body

Bad breath

Your leftover spinach and Brussels sprouts

Highly flexible arms (ducting, hose, extension cords, over-cooked noodles)

Only slime where his heart should be

Hard outer shell (aluminum or plastic)

Lost homework (hidden in guts)

Belly button doubles as a handle

Rubber feet (used for gripping and kicking booty)